THiS
BOOK
BELONGS TO

~~Christina~~

Warner Juvenile Books Edition
Copyright © 1988 by United Feature Syndicate, Inc.
All rights reserved.

Warner Books, Inc., 666 Fifth Avenue, New York, NY 10103
Ⓦ A Warner Communications Company

Printed in the United States of America
First Warner Juvenile Books Printing: March 1988
10 9 8 7 6 5 4 3 2 1

·Christina
BAIARD,

Library of Congress Cataloging-in-Publication Data

Gilchrist, Guy.
    Tiny dinos playing together.

    Summary: The dinosaurs experience feelings of
boredom, curiosity, conceit, happiness, nervousness,
and confidence when they get together to play a game
of baseball.
    [1. Emotions—Fiction.   2. Baseball—Fiction.
3. Dinosaurs—Fiction.   4. Stories in rhyme] I. Title.
PZ8.3.G39Tj 1988   [E]   87-40338
ISBN 1-55782-014-7

FOR MY GOOD FRIEND ROBIN COREY

Guy Gilchrist's
TINY DINOS
PLAYING TOGETHER

A BOOK OF
EVERYDAY FEELINGS

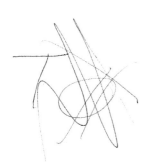

**WARNER
JUVENILE
BOOKS**

A Warner Communications Company

NEW YORK

"Let's get un-bored!"
Plateo roared.
"Let's play a game!"

Bronty was curious.
"A game? What game?
What's its name?"

"Coconut ball!
Coconut ball!
Fun for one, fun for all!
Shake the tree!
Down they fall!
Plenty of coconuts for
coconut ball!"

"Go 'way, Ptery! I'm the hitter!"
selfish Rex said good and loud.

"And *I'm* the greatest
pitcher," said Tot,
very smug and proud.

Bronty was feeling bossy,
so she said with her bossiest face,

"Plateo, you be catcher,
and I will play first base."

Tot and Ptery laughed and played.
They were silly and very excited!

But Rex started feeling guilty
'cause one Dino hadn't been invited.

So while the others played their game
of running, hitting and catching...

Rex searched for Steggie,
the Dino who needed fetching.

If Rex was to hit a home run that day
(a stupendous, tremendous clout),

he wanted *all* his friends to see it —
no one could be left out!

"You *might* strike out," Rex said kindly.
"Why, *I* even struck out once.
But if you'll try," said the generous guy,
"I'll let you share my lunch!"

So Steggie went to bat that day. He was scared and his knees were knocking.

And Triceratot
was confident
as she wound up and
started rocking.

The coconut came
zipping in...

And Steggie's bat went *swish!*

He swung the bat with all his might. He swung and swung but missed.

"Try again," Steggie thought and calmly took a swing...

And you know what?
Steggie hit that ball
over trees and everything!

Rex grinned as hero Steggie
proudly ran the bases.
And there were lots of happy smiles
on lots of Dino faces.